Hedgehug's

Text copyright © 2013 by Dan Pinto
Illustrations copyright © 2013 by Dan Pinto
Library of Congress Cataloging-in-Publication Data is available.
ISBN 978-0-06-196104-5
Typography by Joe Merkel   13 14 15 16 17 SCP 10 9 8 7 6 5 4 3 2 1   ❖   First Edition

Halloween

created & illustrated by
dan pinto

written by
benn sutton

HARPER

An Imprint of HarperCollinsPublishers

Hedgehug the **hedgehog** had **just** put on his **slippers** when he heard someone at the top of his **burrow**.

"Howdy, **pardner!**
Y'all **ready** for the
paaarty?"

"**Hello, Hannah,**"
said Hedgehug.
"**What** party? And
why are you dressed
as a **cowgirl?**"

"Reginald's **Halloween** party!" said Hannah. "Don't **tell** me you **forgot?**"

It was the **biggest** party in the forest, and Hedgehug *had* forgotten all about it.

"I don't even **have** a **costume**," said Hedgehug.

Hedgehug's trunk was full of cool stuff, but nothing seemed right for the party.

"Maybe I can go as a hedgehog," said Hedgehug. "I'm scary."

"Since when?" said Hannah.

Then Hedgehug saw something that just might work.

He slipped his costume carefully over his head.

This is going to be fun, thought Hedgehug.

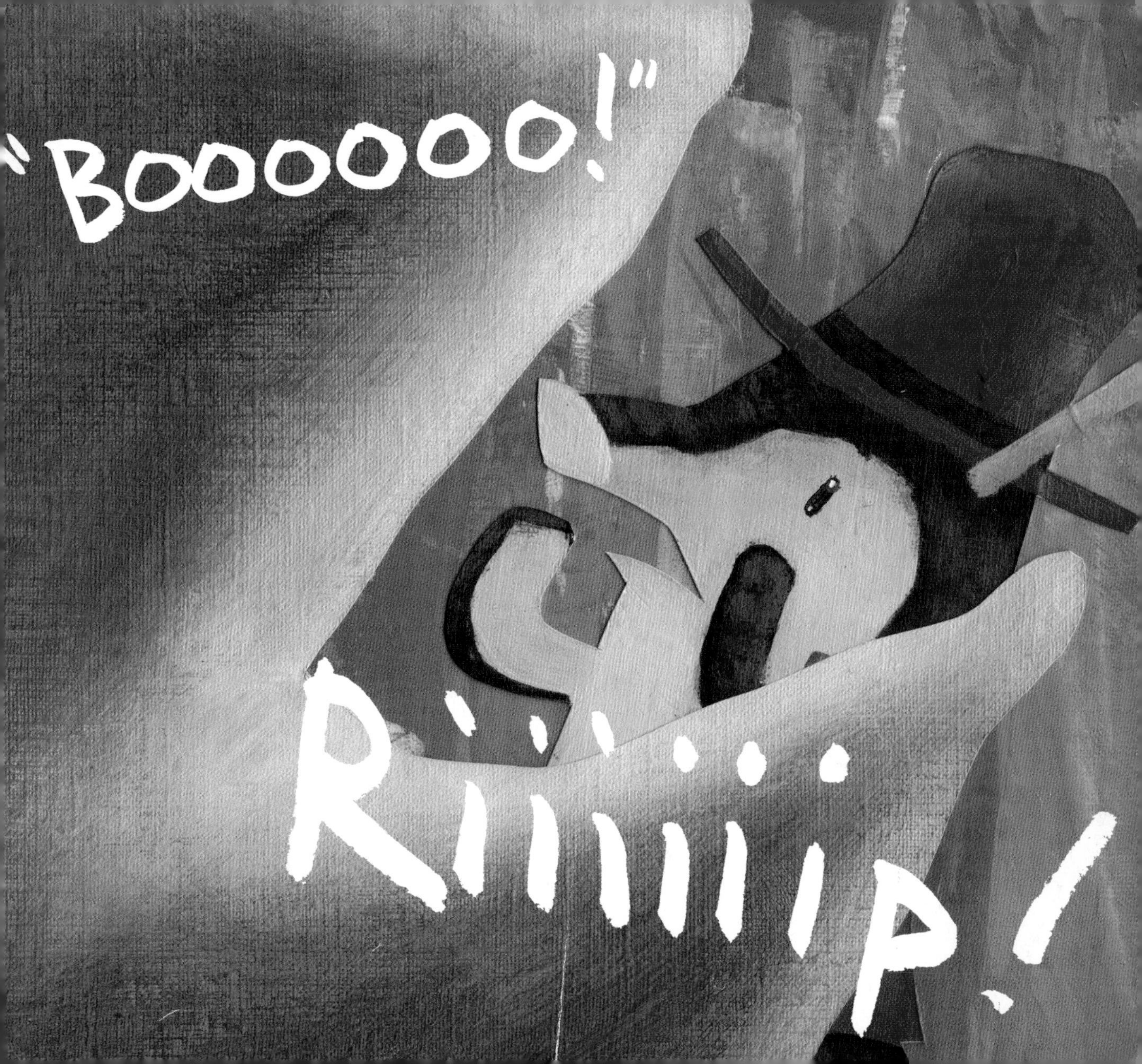
"BOOOOOO!"
RIIIIIIIP!

Hedgehug was **horrified**. *I'm supposed to be a* **ghost**, *not* **Swiss cheese**, he thought.

Luckily
he had **another** idea.

Out in the forest, **night** was falling.
Hedgehug hoped that **Edie**
was **still** in her tree.

What if she'd **already**
left for the party?

"**Wow**," said Hedgehug. "That's a **great** costume."

"I'm glad you like it," said Edie, "or I would have **had** to **turn you into** a **toad**."

"Yes! Make him a toad," said Hannah. "He really needs a costume for the party."

Hedgehug wasn't so sure.

"Do you know any other spells, Edie?" asked Hedgehug.

"I will work some magic," said Edie.

"I need **purple balloons,**

the **leaves** of a **cottonwood** tree,

and a **feather** from a **clever** owl.

Put them together and

Hoot!"

Hedgehug was **so happy** with his costume
he **couldn't** stop smiling.

"**Quick!** Come in," said Doris, putting the **finishing** touches on a **pumpkin.**

"**One** more **minute** and you would have **missed** me."

"Hedgehug," said Doris, "I have a **brilliant idea.**"

Doris got straight to work.

Snip!
clip!
Snip!

CLIP! SNIP! CLIP! Wrap! SNIP!

When she was finished, everyone **agreed**
Hedgehug's costume **was** brilliant...

until

he

tried

to

walk.

Hedgehug picked himself up and waved
good night to his friends.
There was only one place left to go:

home.

Tired, defeated, and **alone,**
Hedgehug **trudged** through the forest,
unaware that **something** was
following him.

Hedgehug **heard** a
sound behind him.

"H-h-hello," said Hedgehug.

"I think the party
is **the other way.**"

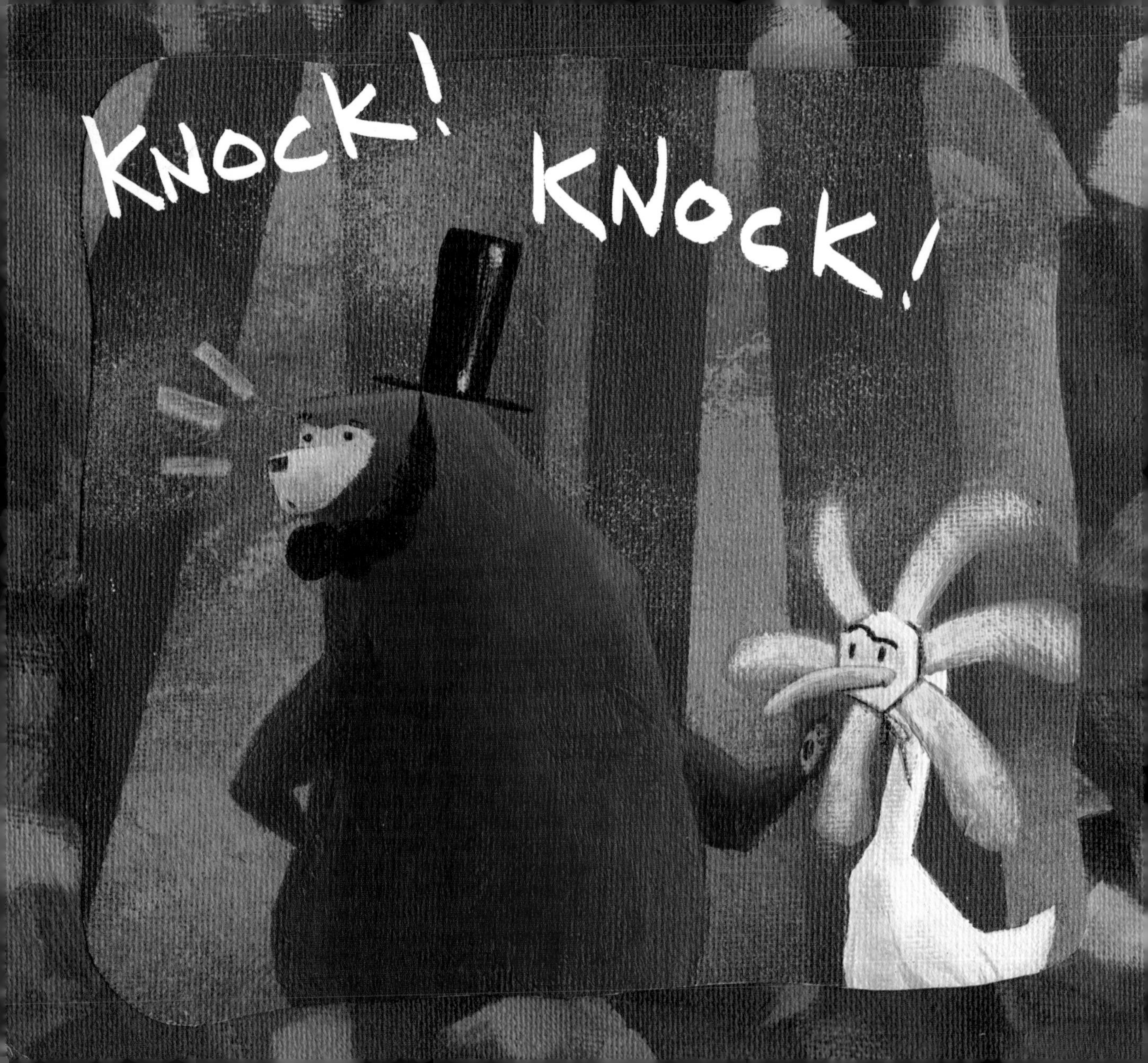
KNOCK!
KNOCK!

"Happy Halloween!" called Hedgehug.

Everyone at the party cheered.

The end

thanks to mk, benn,
joe, and my favorite
roommate, jen.

♡-dan

big thanks to
dan p., mary-kate, jm,
and the handsome reuben.

♡ - benn